The Lucky Pearl

From an Indian folk-tale
Retold by Alfred Könner
Illustrated by Dieter Müller

English text by Helen East

Macdonald

There was once a little Indian girl called Sita who lived in a fishing village. Her job was to look after the hens, but it was impossible to find them enough food.

The sun was so hot the ground was baked hard and the worms hid safely down below.

"Maybe we'll have better luck somewhere else," thought Sita. So she loaded the hens on to a fishing boat and paddled off to see what she could find.

Soon they came to a little island.
The ground was soft and moist and
the worms were fat and succulent.

The hens ate and ate
and ate, and
Sita lay down to
rest and dream.

But the tide came in while Sita was asleep. The waves licked higher, the island grew smaller.

The boat floated gently away and the
hens began to squawk . . .

and Sita woke with a jump. "Save yourselves!" she cried. "Fly home!"

She threw the hens into the air and they clumsily flapped to dry land.

The water was still
rising. "I'll have
to swim for it,"
thought Sita.
But as she stepped
into the sea . . .

SNAP!

An oyster slammed shut on her toe.

The water rose higher, the oyster gripped tighter. Sita wriggled her toe and then, thinking fast, gurgled to the oyster, "Listen, you've a huge pearl inside you!"

“Ooh!” said the oyster. How exciting!”
And it opened up wide to see for
itself. Quick as a flash Sita swam
safely home to the village.

All night Sita dreamt of foolish oysters and beautiful pearls. "Pearls are lucky," she thought. "I think I'll be a pearl diver."

And Sita *was* lucky. She found plenty of oysters and three pearls.

Sita sold the pearls to a travelling trader. He didn't give her a very fair price – only one rupee for the lot –

but it was enough to buy food and oil for Sita and her mother.

When the food was all gone, Sita went diving again. But this time she didn't see a single oyster.

Deeper and deeper she dived, and further and further she swam. Still she found nothing. "Maybe pearls aren't lucky after all," she thought sadly.

But on the way home along the beach,
she suddenly spotted a cluster of
lovely oysters near a big black rock.

Sita scrambled to the top and prepared to dive – then froze in mid-air when she saw . . .

five enormous and deadly sharks hungrily
circling the oyster bed.

"Give up, Sita," warned her mother when she heard about the sharks. "Pearl diving is too dangerous. Maybe you could help the fishermen instead."

"I'm not strong enough
to carry the big fish
they catch," said Sita sadly.

"You'll think
of something,"
comforted
her mother.
"You may be small
but you're clever."

"Yes!" thought Sita. "And the sharks are big, but maybe they aren't so clever." She went back to talk to them.

“Sharks,” she shouted. “You are all big and brave. But who is the boldest of them all? Here is a prize for whoever it may be!” and she threw a stone into the water. Splash!

The sharks were vain. Each one thought, “That prize must be for me!” They rushed at it, jaws open wide.

Crunch! One snapped up the stone, the others snapped into him.

They were all so busy fighting, none of them noticed Sita swimming quietly down . . .

and gathering up armfuls of oysters.

Sita was lucky again. She found only one pearl – but it was enough. A rare and very lucky pink pearl.

This time Sita was determined to get a fair price, so she went to the town to sell her pearl. It was a long, long walk; she arrived very tired, hot and thirsty.

Clutching her pearl tightly in one fist, she sat down under a tree to rest and dream in the cool shade.

Sita woke with a jump. The pearl was gone! Stolen away while she slept! "Why am I so unlucky?" she sobbed.

"Don't cry," said a voice. "Here is your pearl. I saw you drop it in your sleep, so I looked after it for you."

The boy twisted some grasses together, knotted them round the pearl, then slipped the band over Sita's hair. "Now your pearl will be safe," he said.

Sita walked happily on through the town, the pink pearl glowing on her forehead.

Suddenly she heard a fanfare of trumpets and voices shouting, "Make way for the royal elephant!" And sitting proudly on the elephant's back was the boy who'd found her pearl.

"Listen," he cried. "A royal announcement!
The King is dying without an heir,
so his wise old elephant
must pick out the next
ruler from amongst us all!"

Everyone crowded up to the elephant; rich and poor, old and young – all hoped they would be chosen.

But the elephant ignored them.
He looked straight at Sita who was standing quietly aside. Then he trumpeted loud and clear, and dropped a garland around her neck.

"Hooray!" cried the boy and "Hooray!" roared the crowd. "Long live our new ruler, Princess Lucky Pearl."

"Sometimes dreams do come true," she said. "And pearls are lucky after all."